To my family

© Tramuntana Editorial, 2017
© Text and Illustrations: Maria Girón

Original title: *Arturo y el elefante sin memoria*

Translation rights arranged by IMC Agència Literària, SL

First English edition
Published by Flyaway Books, Louisville, Kentucky

21 22 23 24 25 26 27 28 29 30–10 9 8 7 6 5 4 3 2 1

Book design by Allison Taylor
Text set in Brandon Grotesque and Might Could Pencil

Library of Congress Cataloging-in-Publication Data
Names: Girón, Maria, 1983- author, illustrator.
Title: Arthur and the forgetful elephant / story and art by Maria Girón.
Other titles: Arturo y el elefante sin memoria. English
Description: First English edition. | Louisville, Kentucky : Flyaway Books, 2020. | Audience: Ages 3-7. | Audience: Grades K-1. | Summary: Arthur helps a sad and forgful elephant rediscover his memory by distracting him with fun and games.
Identifiers: LCCN 2020002207 (print) | LCCN 2020002208 (ebook) | ISBN 9781947888272 (hardback) | ISBN 9781611649963 (ebook)
Subjects: CYAC: Elephants--Fiction. | Memory--Fiction. | Friendship--Fiction.
Classification: LCC PZ7.1.G5838 Ar 2020 (print) | LCC PZ7.1.G5838 (ebook) | DDC [E]--dc23
LC record available at https://lccn.loc.gov/2020002207
LC ebook record available at https://lccn.loc.gov/2020002208

PRINTED IN CHINA

Most Flyaway Books are available at special quantity discounts when purchased in bulk by corporations, organizations, and special-interest groups. For more information, please e-mail SpecialSales@flyawaybooks.com.

Arthur and the Forgetful Elephant

story and art by

Maria Girón

Is it raining? Arthur thought.
But it's sunny!
Then he looked up.

"Hi, up there!" he called.
"My name's Arthur.
What's yours?"

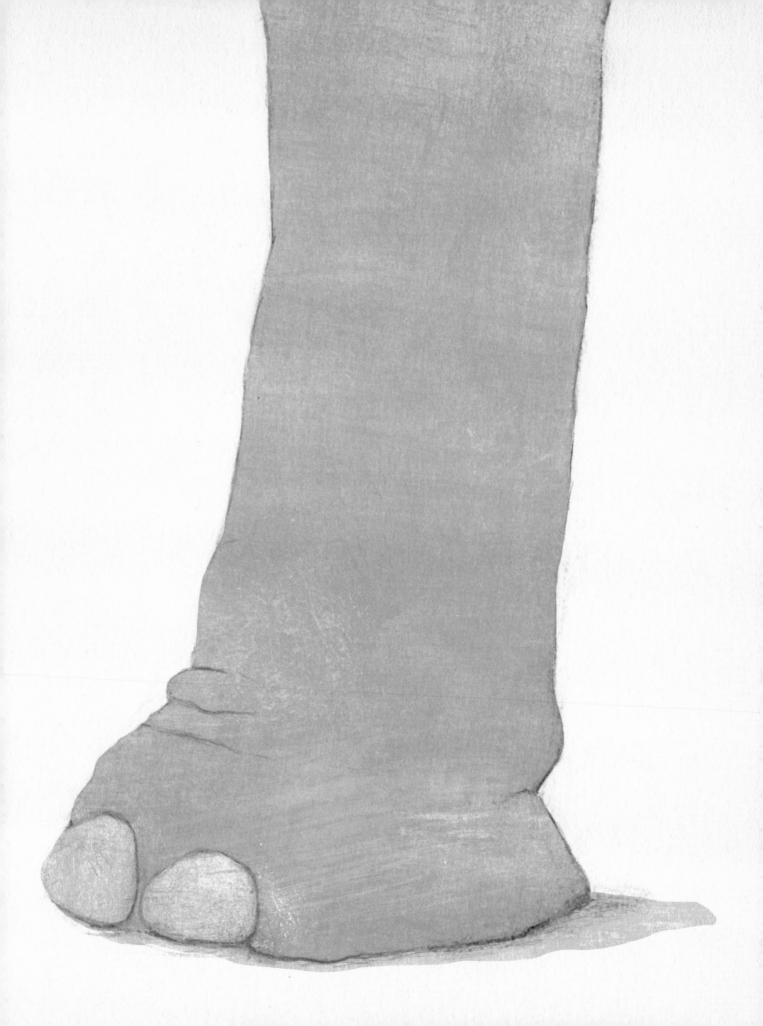

"I forget," sobbed the elephant.
"You do?" Arthur asked.
"Yes! I can't remember who I am
or where I live or . . . anything!"

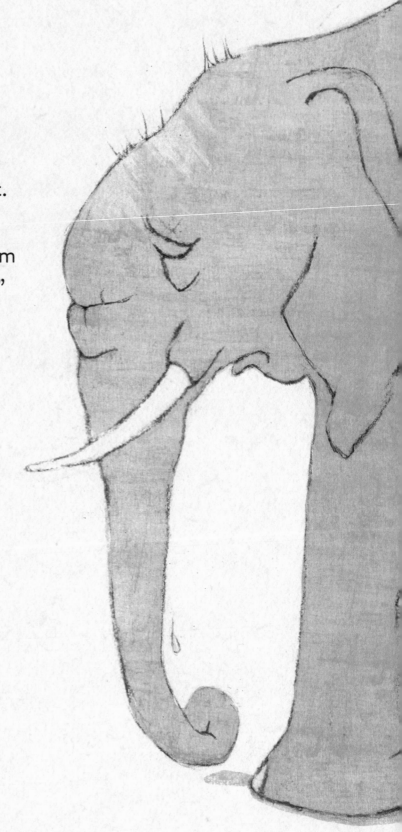

Arthur thought, Sometimes I forget where my toys are.

Where's my
helicopter?

And I forgot my lines in the school play.

But what if I forgot really important things?

If I forgot EVERYTHING,
I'd be sad
and lonely
and scared.

Poor elephant.

"Maybe I can help!"

"Know what I do when I'm upset?" said Arthur.
"I try to think about something else until I feel better."
"And then your problems go away?" asked the elephant.
"No, but they feel smaller," said Arthur.
"You'll see. Come on, let's play!"

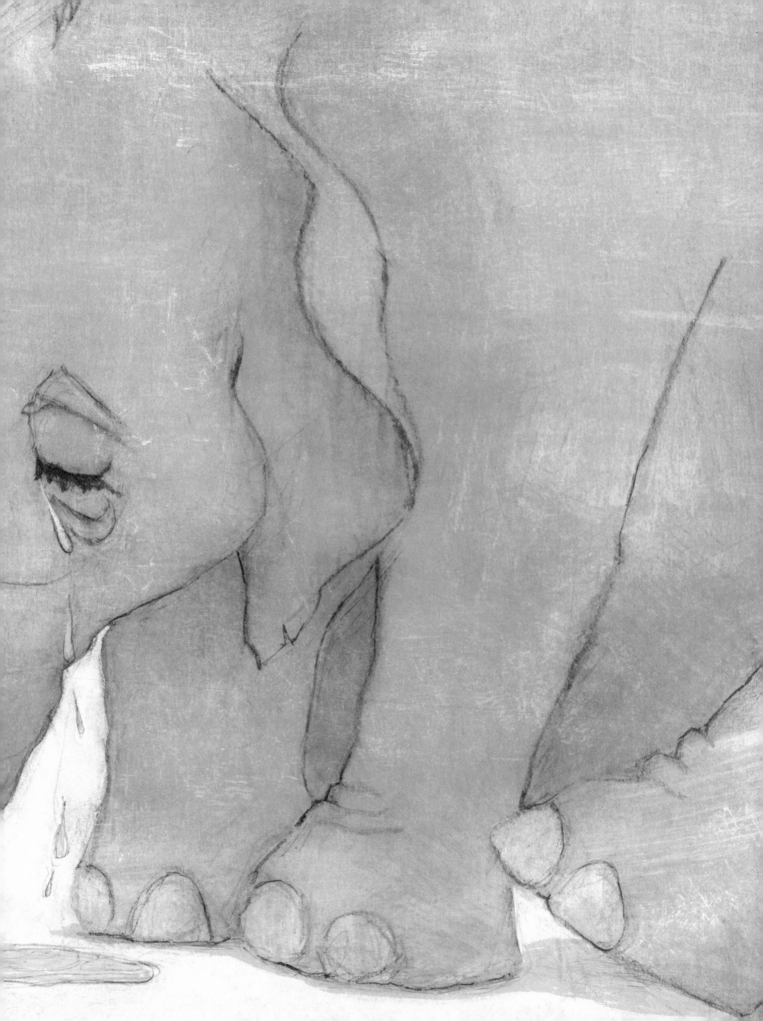

And off they went.

1, 2, 3 . . .

Arthur and the elephant had stopped for a snack when . . .

Arthur saw his friends.

Yes! Come draw with us!

They played and played
until the sun began to set.

And then the elephant remembered—just a little bit.

Family? I think I have a family! But where are they?

Slowly, the elephant started to remember a little more.
I do have a family! I have to find them!

Baroooo!

BaROOha!

BaaaaROOOOhaaaa!

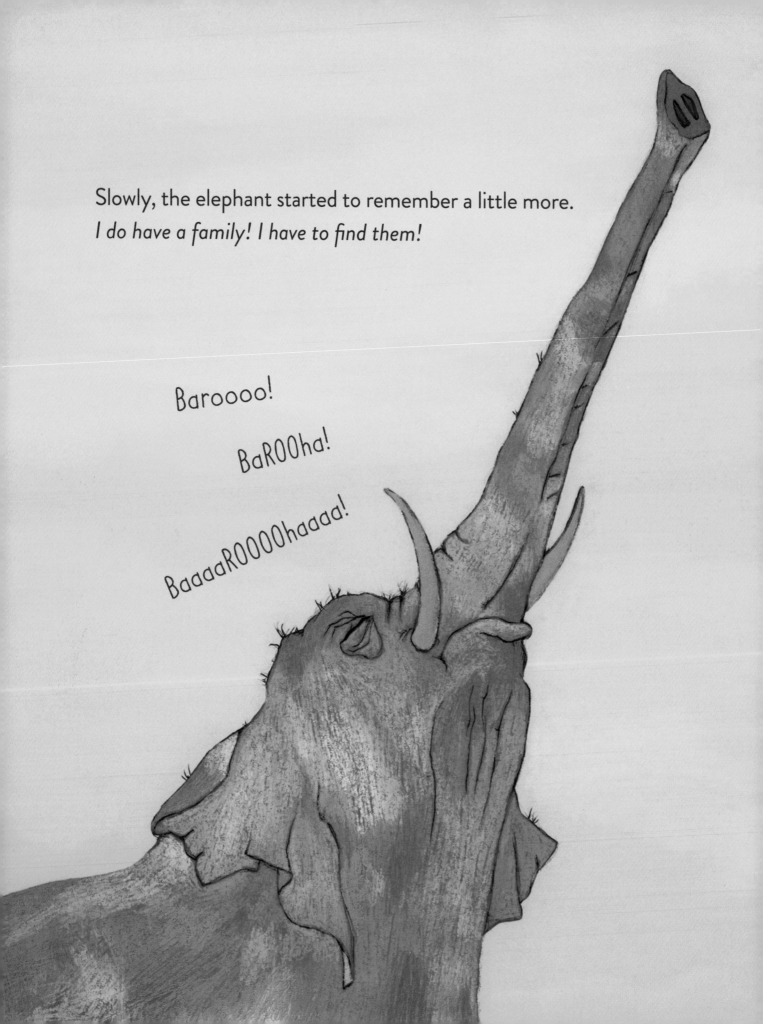

Then he waited for a very long time, until . . .

"Thank you for helping me remember, dear Arthur,"
said the elephant. "Will I see you tomorrow?"
"Yes!" Arthur said. "And the next day,
and the next day, and the next!"

And with that, the new friends said good night.